SUPPOSE YOU MET A WITCH

BY IAN SERRAILLIER

ILLUSTRATED BY ED EMBERLEY

LITTLE, BROWN AND COMPANY
BOSTON, TORONTO

Library of Congress Cataloging in Publication Data

Serraillier, Ian.
  Suppose you met a witch.
  SUMMARY: Relates in verse how Roland and Miranda
handled the situation when they were trapped in a
sack by a witch.
  The text was first published in 1952 in a collection
of poems entitled Belinda and the swans.
  [1. Witches—Fiction. 2. Stories in rhyme]
I. Emberley, Ed, illus. II. Title.
PZ8.3.S47Su3   75-105751
ISBN 0-316-78125-8   [E]

Suppose You Met a Witch was first published in a collection of poems entitled
Belinda and the Swans by Ian Serraillier, Jonathan Cape Ltd., London, 1952.

FIRST EDITION   T 09/73   PRINTED IN THE UNITED STATES OF AMERICA

Suppose you met a witch . . . There's one I know,
all willow-gnarled and whiskered head to toe.
We drownded her at Ten Foot Bridge
last June, I think —
but I've seen her often since at twilight time
under the willows by the river brink,
skimming the wool-white meadow mist
astride her broom o' beech.

And once, as she flew past, with a sudden twist
and flick of the stick she whisked me in
head over heels, splash in the scummy water
up to my chin —
ugh! . . .

Yet there are witless folk will say
they don't exist.

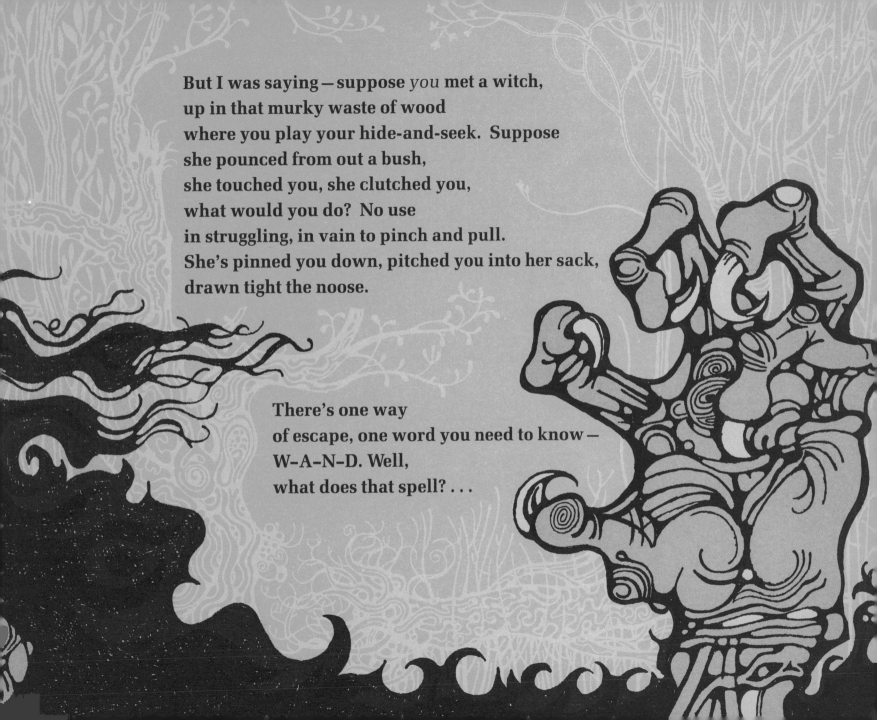

But I was saying—suppose *you* met a witch,
up in that murky waste of wood
where you play your hide-and-seek. Suppose
she pounced from out a bush,
she touched you, she clutched you,
what would you do? No use
in struggling, in vain to pinch and pull.
She's pinned you down, pitched you into her sack,
drawn tight the noose.

There's one way
of escape, one word you need to know—
W–A–N–D. Well,
what does that spell? . . .

They learned it years ago,
two children—Roland and Miranda—clapped
in a witch's sack and trapped
just as you might be. *He*
was a mild and dreamy boy, musical
as a lark—in the dark
of the jolting sack he sang. *She*
was quick in all she did, a nimble wit, her brain
busy as a hive of bees at honey time.

And Grimblegrum — that was the witch's name —
jogged them home.

This was the usual sort, a candy villa
with walls of gingerbread, porch and pillar
of barley sugar. She kicked the gate
and the licorice-beaded door,
undid the sack string and tipped them
onto the glassy glacier-minted floor.

As Roland fell, his boot struck
the crystal paving stones and chipped them.
Like an angry rocket
she launched at him. Miranda
sprang for the magic wand
and pinched it from her pocket.

"Tip, tap — O house of cake,
be a cloud-reflecting lake
with me and Roland, each a swan,
gracefully afloat thereon!
And, deeper than e'er plummet sounded,
Grimblegrum the witch be drownded!"

'Twas done—
look there, d'you see two swans
a-gliding, serene and cool
upon that heaven-painted pool,
over the blue sky, over the floating clouds that shine
like snow-white fleeces?

Sudden, in burst of bubbles the witch popped up
and shivered the clouds to pieces.
"I'll gobble you yet!" she gulped,
but all she gobbled was water as with windmill arms
she thrashed and lashed at them. No swimmer,
she would have sunk like a boulder below,

had not a felon crow,
black-hearted as his feather, swooping, dipping,
hoisted her by the belt and borne her, boggy,
drooping, dripping,
home.

"She'll follow us — no time to lose —
quick, we must fly!" Miranda cried.
Heavily they rose;
far over field and forest, with whining wing
all night through
till dawn of day they flew.

Meanwhile the Grimble-witch, now dry,
had put on her seven-league boots and (do or die)
seven miles at a step came galloping,
gulping, "Gobble you yet, I'll gobble you yet!"

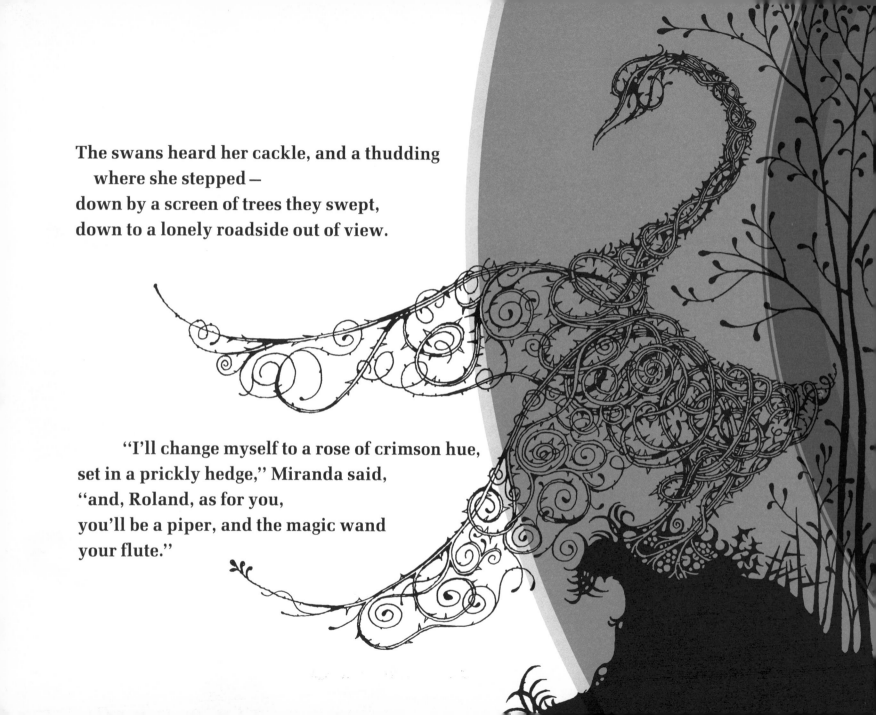

The swans heard her cackle, and a thudding
    where she stepped —
down by a screen of trees they swept,
down to a lonely roadside out of view.

"I'll change myself to a rose of crimson hue,
set in a prickly hedge," Miranda said,
"and, Roland, as for you,
you'll be a piper, and the magic wand
your flute."

Not a second too soon — for the witch's boot
touched ground beside them. And she croaked:

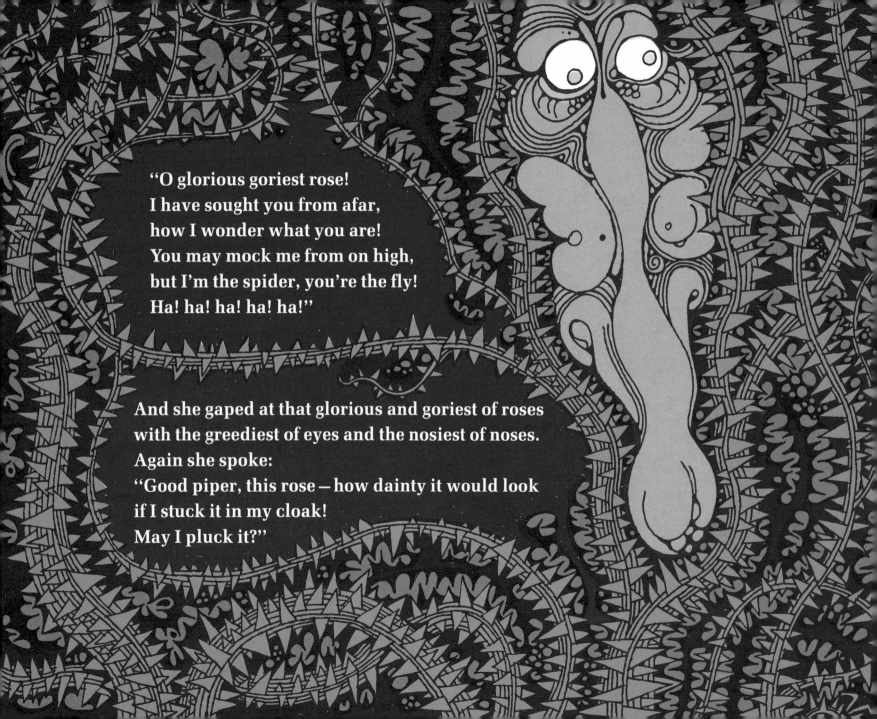

"O glorious goriest rose!
I have sought you from afar,
how I wonder what you are!
You may mock me from on high,
but I'm the spider, you're the fly!
Ha! ha! ha! ha! ha!"

And she gaped at that glorious and goriest of roses
with the greediest of eyes and the nosiest of noses.
Again she spoke:
"Good piper, this rose—how dainty it would look
if I stuck it in my cloak!
May I pluck it?"

"Good lady, you may. And I'll play
to you the while." And Roland smiled,
for his was a *magic* flute,
each golden note entrancing—
none could listen without dancing.

One note one,
she spun like a top.

Two notes two,
she hopped and couldn't stop.

Three notes three —
and into that thorny thistle-y tree
with a hop, skip and a jump went she.

Tootle-toot! sang the flute
and up went her boot
and down again soon
to the tantivy tune.
Every thorn and twig
did dance to the jig
and the witch willy-nilly —
each prickle and pin
as it skewered her in
was driving her silly.

"Hi!
    Ho!"
        shrieked she,
and "Tickle-me-thistle!" and "Prickle-de-dee!"
And battered she was as she trotted and tripped,
and her clothes were torn and tattered and ripped
till at last,
all mingled and mangled,
    her right leg entangled,
        her left leg right-angled,
firm as a prisoner pinned to the mast,
she
        stuck
            fast.

Silence, not a sound as Roland wiped
the sweat from his brow. Then gently with his pipe
he touched the rose. Out leaped Miranda
to the ground. Hand in hand,
chuckling, through the wild wood
away home they ran.

That same evening, a cowman passing by
paused by a roadside bush to cut a switch.
He heard a cry;
turning, saw in a hedge nearby a prickly witch
who screamed and yelled and hissed at him and spat.

So he put a match to the hedge.   And that was that.